Party Time!

Marie Miller

Rosen Classroom Books & Materials™
New York

It is Dad's birthday.
We are going to have
a party today!

At 1:00, Mom and I make a cake.

At 2:00, I wrap the gifts.

At 3:00, I make a sign.

At 4:00, I blow up balloons.

At 5:00, we hide!
Here comes Dad!

Happy birthday, Dad!